FOR VICTORIA

AND SARA

Library of Congress Cataloging-in-Publication Data available.

ISBN 978-1-4521-4401-6

Manufactured in China.

MIX
Paper from
responsible sources
FSC
www.fsc.org    FSC™ C008047

Design by Sara Gillingham Studio.
Typeset in Bernhard Gothic and True North.
The illustrations in this book were pieced together with this and that.

10 9 8 7 6 5 4 3 2 1

Chronicle Books LLC
680 Second Street
San Francisco, California 94107

Chronicle Books—we see things differently.
Become part of our community at www.chroniclekids.com.

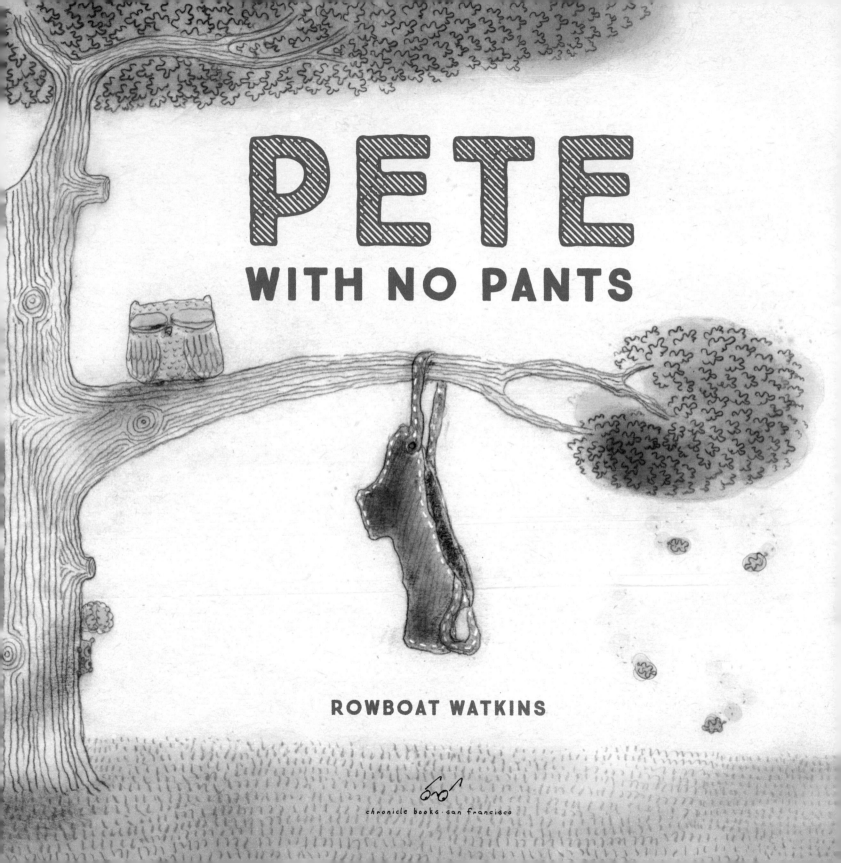

# PETE
## WITH NO PANTS

### ROWBOAT WATKINS

chronicle books · san francisco

Shortly after breakfast, Pete decided he was a boulder.

KNOCK!
KNOCK!
KNOCK!

SOMEONE
HAS
TO SAY
"WHO'S
THERE?"

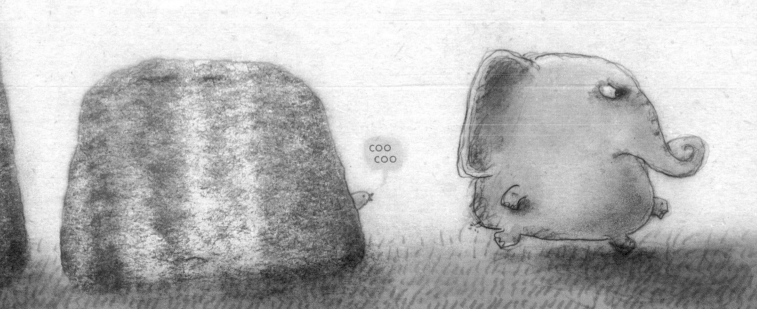

Soon Pete had a better idea.

LET'S SEE... I'M **GRAY.** CHECK.

I'M **NUTS** ABOUT ACORNS. CHECK.

AND I'M **NOT** WEARING **PANTS.**

YUP! I'M A SQUIRREL!

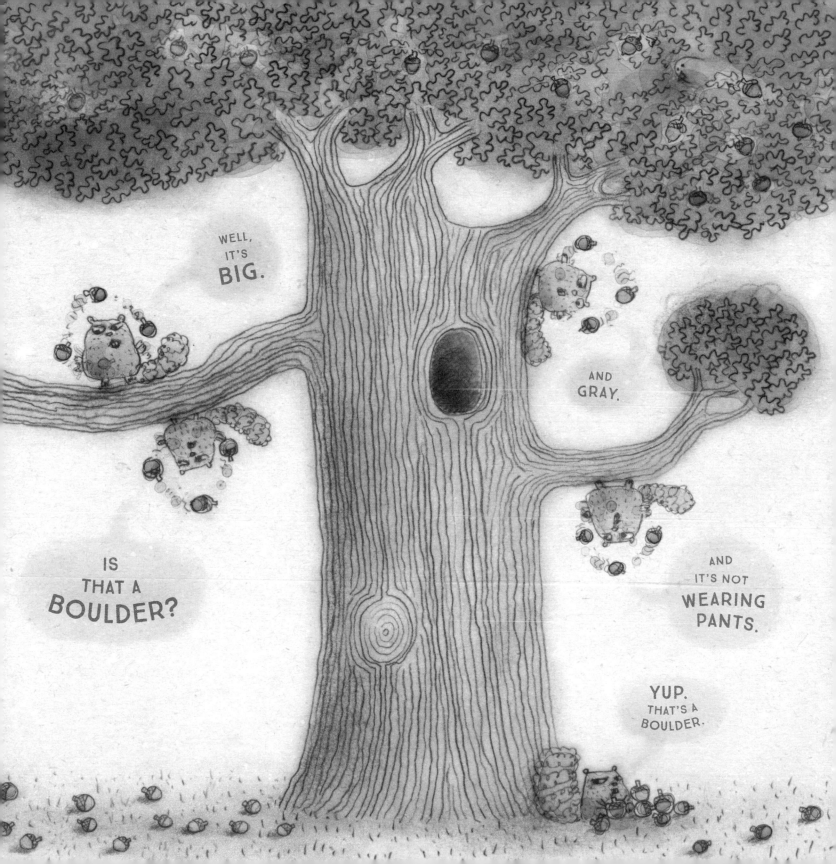

Next morning was cloudy.

LET'S SEE . . .
I'M GRAY.
CHECK.

AND
PUFFY.
CHECK.

AND . . .

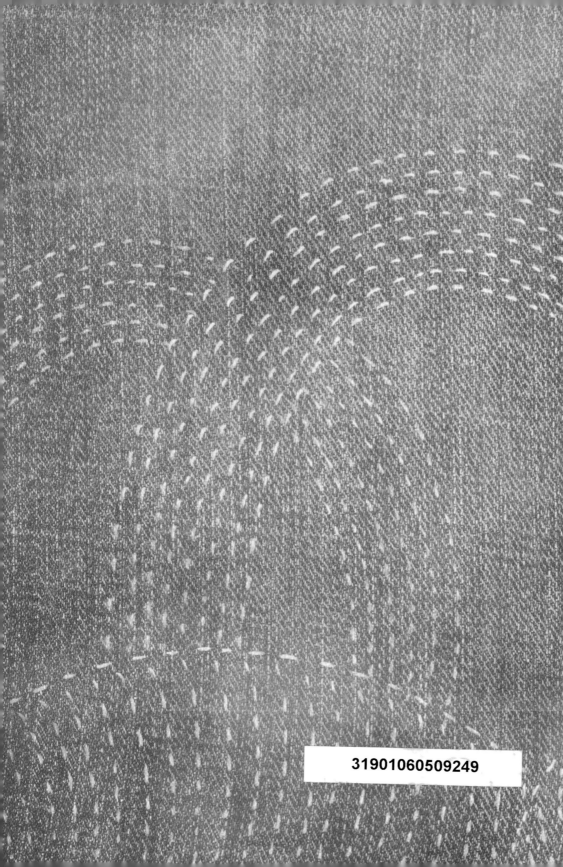

31901060509249